Lucas Comes to America

Lovingly Translated By
Carolyn Farb

AuthorHouse™
1663 Liberty Drive
Bloomington, IN 47403
www.authorhouse.com
Phone: 1-800-839-8640

ISBN: 978-1-4567-4541-7

Printed in the United States by BookMasters, Inc
30 Amberwood Parkway Ashland OH 44805
April 2011
M8412

Any people depicted in stock imagery provided by Thinkstock are models,
and such images are being used for illustrative purposes only.
Certain stock imagery © Thinkstock.

This book is printed on acid-free paper.

Because of the dynamic nature of the Internet, any web addresses or links contained in
this book may have changed since publication and may no longer be valid. The views
expressed in this work are solely those of the author and do not necessarily reflect the
views of the publisher, and the publisher hereby disclaims any responsibility for them.

authorHOUSE®

Caroline and Lucas

Mam's Farm in Manchester, England

Airplanes and America

I was just a little pup living on my Mam's farm in Manchester, England, when a man named Dick came to visit. Mam took wonderful care of all of us. She breeds Lucas terriers. A famous British war hero named Sir Jocelyn Lucas crossbred Sealyhams and Norfolk terriers to create us. All Lucas terriers are born with black hair. When we lose our baby black hair, our true color blossoms. We come in several shades—I'm tan.

I soon learned that the man named Dick had come to choose the perfect pup to bring to his friend in America. After a few days, Dick made his decision; he chose me!

Dick and Mam looked around the farmhouse for a carrier he could use to transport me on the airplane. They found something they thought would be suitable, but when we got to the airport, the lady in the blue uniform didn't like my carrier. She said it was too big and wouldn't fit under the seat, so we had to turn around and go back to the farm to search for a new one. Mam and Dick went shopping and found a backpack that seemed to work best. I wasn't very big—only five pounds. I could even poke my head out of the top of it!

The next day, we drove back to the airport. This time, the lady in blue gave us permission to board the plane. During the flight, Dick told me that we were going to Texas and assured me that I would love it. He said I was going to live with his friend, a nice lady named Caroline who was looking forward to welcoming me into her home.

When the plane landed, I knew I would be meeting her soon. As we left the airport, I noticed that everything in Texas seemed so different to a little guy like me who had come from a quaint farm in England.

We arrived at Caroline's home, and there she was, standing on her doorstep eagerly waiting to swoop me up in her arms. I immediately sensed I was finally home, but there was a sadness about Caroline. She had lost her beloved child, Jake, four years ago. More recently, she had lost her dearest pet, Bogie, a handsome Shih Tzu. Theirs were really big shoes for me to fill. I thought to myself, *if she gives me half a chance, I'll try to make her smile.*

On My Way to Texas with Dick

I'm Caroline's Bundle of Joy

The Basics and Beyond

From the beginning, I could tell that Caroline was the artsy type. You might even say that I'm now officially "an art dog." Caroline has helped artists all her life — it's just one of her many passions. Living at Caroline's is like living in a small museum. Right from the start, I intuitively knew what was hands-off and what I should admire only from afar. Today, that no-touch policy still prevails.

I quickly learned the rules in my new home: no chewing, no raising my leg, no massive puppy destruction. When Caroline is busy and I'm left to my own devices, I have a lot of fun toys to play with. One of my favorites is a shoe that squeaks a lot. They say that if you give a dog a shoe, he won't be able to tell the difference between his toy shoe and a real shoe, but I can.

Each day, I decide which toys I want to play with and where I want to hide them. You'll never guess where one of my favorite places is—it's under Mom's bed! The dust ruffle around the bed makes it look like a cave. I enjoy giving those toys a tough time, tugging until the stuffing comes loose.

When Caroline is putting on her makeup, occasionally she drops a Q-tip, which is usually saturated with a delicious cream. I love taking it to my secret hiding place! This gets me in big trouble though because the ingredients in those cosmetics can make me sick. Caroline watches over me.

Super Sleuth Caroline

Carl, Ugh – the Dog Trainer and His Wall of Champions

In fact, she looks out for me in a lot of ways. When I first arrived, Caroline thought it would be a good idea for me to work with a well-known pet trainer named Carl. Unfortunately, he was very rigid and had no consideration for my feelings. The only effect of the training was that I became extremely frustrated. Mom was smart enough to pick up on that. Like I said, she looks out for me— she's my love bunny.

Caroline and Ana, my amazing housekeeper and nanny, took matters into their own hands and started training me themselves. I was so glad to be rid of Carl that I was ready to jump through hoops. We raced through the basics, and soon I was self-housetrained. Victory!

That was simple compared to getting my diet straight. We all have our different tastes when it comes to food. Caroline spent a lot of time trying to figure out what was best for my diet and what I should eat. We've got it down pat now. I prefer dry food. With canned food, there's no crunch factor. Mom and Ana also understand my preference not to dine alone. Company always makes food taste better.

Not only do I love Caroline and Ana, but I also love my new home. It's really fun to go out in the backyard and search for rats and lizards, things I shouldn't eat, and bark at the dog next door to let him know who the boss is. The whirling pool sweeper will always be Enemy Number One. It has a long tail that I find simply irresistible. There were so many imaginary duels until my Mom outwitted me and set it on a timer. Now it goes off when I'm sleeping!

There are other things I like to sample around the house. Caroline has a collection of beautiful butterflies. She gathers them when they land on our porch and then artfully places them on an end table by the sofa. Occasionally, I give into the temptation of putting my paw on top of the mound of butterflies and playing with them. Did you know that Lucas terriers have large paws for small dogs?

Butterflies - My Favorites

Will I Always Be Number One?

Routines and Research

When Caroline goes out in the evening, she leaves the television on the cartoon channel so I don't get lonesome. I love the bright colors, the animated voices, and the music. After a reasonable amount of time has passed, I go and wait patiently by the front door for her return, listening for the sound of the gate opening. When she finally opens the door, I besiege her for a treat and a walk.

I get exhausted just watching Caroline. I wonder where that woman gets her energy. Is it from her fizzy Vitamin C drinks? She stays up much later than I do watching all those old Turner Classics. She's a real movie buff. We usually watch old movies late into the night, and when the movies are over, I walk up the magic staircase that takes me up onto Caroline's bed. I have short legs, so there's no way I could climb up onto that high bed on my own. We then snuggle, say my prayers, and it's lights out.

Caroline says my internal clock is always on schedule. When morning comes, I stand tall and look right into her eyes! If she doesn't stir, then I start talking to her until she gets up. It's not that I have any great need to go outside; it's just time to get up and start another wonderful day!

Some mornings I like to sit on the mat just outside the back door and feel the fresh dew on my face, listening to the sounds of the morning. The leaves that fall from the neighbor's trees often catch my eye, as will the dance of the sprinklers when they come on. Doing my business comes later and at my leisure. In fact, I tend to do everything on my own terms—the terrier way.

When I go outside, I prefer the bushes and patches of Confederate jasmine for taking care of my business, and now and then, I pick up a few bugs. That makes me really itchy, so Caroline gives me an allergy pill. At first, she was frustrated when she couldn't get me to take the pill, but then she realized I have no humility when it involves treats. She found these yummy Pill Pockets made of real chicken! Whoever invented those sure did their research. Caroline puts the pill in the pocket and rolls it into a ball, and I take it like a champ!

The inventor of the Pill Pocket should give some advice to the designers who make clothes for four-legged creatures. In all modesty, I've been told I'm a handsome chap. I'm sleek, with a bit of a girth, and weigh in consistently at 17.5 pounds. I'm a hard body to die for. One of my Mom's friends gave me a festive red jacket for the holidays. I didn't want to insult him, but it felt like a straightjacket—I couldn't move! It would be so much better for all concerned if the Velcro was on the top side. There wouldn't be quite the stress and struggle when getting dressed.

Tossing the Shoe as My Fur Flies

A Visit to Dr. Jensen

Romance and Trips to the Vet

Being a romantic chap, I started thinking about having a family of my own. My choices were limited. There aren't many prospects around here except for Zoe, my Lucas terrier neighbor. When I first saw her, I thought, *she's beautiful! Just imagine—a little Lucas*. I didn't know the ropes on our first try, but neither did she. We were novices and hoped for good results. My Mom thought a pup I could call my own would be good company for me. At the same time, she worries that I might not be that generous about sharing my space. After all, I've been master of our home for four years now.

Over the years, I've become more comfortable with going to the vet for my checkups. Dr. Jensen is strictly business. In fact, he's very busy and has lots of clients. His main goal is to get everyone in and out—he's not one for small talk.

The other day when we went for my regular checkup, I darted off as soon as we walked into the office. Mom couldn't figure out where I was headed; she didn't realize that I already knew the drill. I was just getting the process started. First, I dashed to the scale to get weighed. Next, the nurse put me up on the big table. Then, Dr. Jensen looked at me, poked me, and took my temperature. I had a feeling a shot was forthcoming, and Mom was given some pills for me to take home. Sound fun?

Dr. Jensen is always there when we need him and is sensitive to the fact that my Mom thinks of me like her son, not a canine.

Hurricanes and Hotels

We had a hurricane this past season. The winds howled, and the houses and trees fell like pick-up sticks. All the electricity went out, and we didn't have water for drinking, cooking, or bathing. It was very hot because there was no air-conditioning. The everyday things we take for granted were no longer available.

During the hurricane, Mom and I bravely stayed our course at home. After it passed, we lived uncomfortably for several days. We felt like pioneers in the wilderness. Finally, Mom and I decided to go to a hotel. It was a two-fold challenge: first, trying to find a hotel that had space available, and second, finding one that was animal friendly. We finally found the perfect place.

Before we arrived at the hotel, Mom had a serious talk with me because I like to bark at almost everything. It's my nature to be protective. She told me they would throw us out if I barked every time someone walked past our hotel door. I listened to her this time, and we ended up staying there for about ten days.

Captain Mysterious

I liked it there because the nice bellmen would take me for walks downtown; it felt like an adventure walking amidst the broken glass. The hotel people went the extra mile. They even had dog dishes and special food for their pet guests. Under the circumstances, they did everything they could to make everyone feel at home. One of the men who lived in the condo part of the hotel walked around with a parrot on his shoulder in a floral print shirt. He was very strange and quite a sight to behold. I was sad when it was time to leave, but home is where my heart is!

Now every time we have a power surge, I shake and I bark at the thunder, hoping to make it go away. Just in case there's another big storm, we keep flashlights and a supply of candles nearby.

Lucas Dancing with the Dragonflies

Walking, Water, and When to Listen

I always give a nod to Zoe's home next door when I'm out on my walk. I'm sure she senses my presence. When I stop to visit, her mother likes to give me treats. Just between us, the treats don't taste so good—they're organic. They made me sick the last time I took her up on her offer. So the next time I went over, I graciously declined. Mom has always told me not to take food from strangers. What may be good for other dogs may not be good for me.

When we go walking, it's fun to run into other dogs. Everyone admires my jaunty gait—attributed to the great actor Charlie Chaplin. Thinking of myself as king of the road, I wait for their approach and lie down in the grass. Frankly, I don't know what I would do if one of those big dogs took me up on my bark. Mostly, I like to sniff, chase birds and squirrels, and dance with dragonflies.

Many of my canine friends like to swim. Our house has a big pool in the backyard, but swimming is not a high priority for me. A friend of my Mom's took me in the pool one day when I was just a wee pup so that I would know how to get out in case I ever fell in. I didn't enjoy the experience and haven't ventured back since.

I Love Being Pampered

I'm not completely opposed to water. In fact, after I've had the opportunity to play explorer in the neighborhood, there's nothing better than a luxurious bath by Ana. When you're low to the ground, you're a collector of garbage. People litter, and I'm a perfect example of someone who has to walk among that trash. What can we do about these litterbugs? After my bath, Ana wraps me up in a big towel and blows my hair dry so I don't catch a cold. Mom even gets a special conditioner from the groomer that makes my hair very silky. I love the feeling of being held.

There was a lady groomer who used to come to our house in a big van. She was nothing like Ana. When trimming my nails one day, the groomer actually drew blood—and it hurt! My Mom finally figured out that there was a problem when she noticed me running and hiding under her bed whenever the groomer came. The lady pretended my behavior was normal. She thought she could fool my Mom, but I have my ways of letting her know when something isn't as it should be. Caroline eventually picked up on the hints I gave her. It's so important for parents to pay close attention and be sensitive to those they love.

Finding the Best Dish for Me

Visitors and Valiance

Caroline is very involved in a number of projects to help others—in education, the arts, the medical field, preservation, and of course, animal rights that look after my constituency. There are many interesting people who visit us on different occasions. She's gracious about opening our home.

When Caroline's friends come over, most of them are happy to see me. I've had an unfavorable vibe only a couple of times, and I felt it in an instant. You might say the hairs on my back literally stood up. I really frightened those individuals with my growls and posturing. The only other time I go into a defense mode is when Mom and I are watching a show and I hear a dog barking on the television. They sound as though they're right there in the bedroom with us!

Back to Mom's visitors, my other pet peeve is when someone comes into our home and totally ignores me—that is a lack of manners. I wonder where they were brought up. I won't allow that to happen, as I am a significant family member in this household.

I realize I have to share Caroline with the world. When she has to travel, a lady named Lorraine house-sits. She's like a grandmother to me. She wears funny T-shirts with dogs on them and always brings me a super surprise—a toy to die for. She's very much in demand, and we have to book her well in advance. I'm her favorite—at least that's what she tells me. I hope none of the other pooches who read this book get too jealous.

Lorraine understands me, but not everyone does—especially children five and under. They seem to think we're on the same playing field. Don't they know that everything from the doorknobs down is mine? Just the other day, Kirin, my Mom's niece, was visiting, and she put all of her toys in my special house. In fact, she got in there herself! It was a tight squeeze! With that said, there is something I appreciate about Kirin. She always remembers to say thank you. Some big people could learn from her. When people do something nice for you, they're doing it from the heart, so showing appreciation is well received.

Manners are very important, and so is remembering to follow the rules. In our neighborhood, I'm a guy who follows the rules—which means I stay on-leash. The other day, Caroline bravely stopped a macho man who was strutting about with two big dogs and no leash. She reminded him that someone could get hurt because of him not following the rules. Recently, a small poodle had been injured by someone's unpredictable pet that was off-leash.

My Kingdom

Though I like to follow the rules, I do have my moments. The very mention of the words "leash" and "walk" gets my juices flowing, and I'm ready to take off at a moment's notice. Mom never thought she'd have to spell in front of a pup like me. Well, she never had a Lucas terrier before. We're highly intelligent.

The other night, I got the hungries, and Caroline tried to play possum—you know, pretending she was asleep. Like I said, we're smart dudes. I did not relent. She gets very unnerved when I start the barking routine. I can't help myself, because I'm so excited about life! I've heard her say to her friends on more than one occasion that she's worried a neighbor might try to give me a poison biscuit to silence my bark. I'll just have to take that risk.

What I'm concerned about more than that is someone coming into Caroline's life full-time—you know, like a significant other. She reassures me that if that does happen, he has to understand that I'm in the picture big-time and forever; it's a package deal, the two of us. You have to consider these matters in advance.

Caroline constantly reminds me that I'm a favorite son, a loving companion, and a loyal protector.

Much to my pride, Zoe and I received the good news—that we were going to become parents! Well, she had two fine sons, and we decided to share them. My son's name is Maximillian or "Maxi Taxi" for short.

I look forward to telling you more about my son in my next book: *Along Came Maxi.*

The Barking Brigade: Maximilian and Lucas

My story is for kids and grownups alike – the young at heart. We dedicate this book to the memory of Carolyn's son, Jake Kenyon Shulman, and all the beloved canines – Bogie, Charcoal, Prince and Charley –who have given unconditional love.

Sofía van der Dys

The Family Christmas Card